For Lucy,
Joseph and William

A.McA.

For Heidi.
It's good to have you home!

D.H.

First published in Great Britain in 2008 by

Gullane Children's Books

185 Fleet Street, London, EC4A 2HS

www.gullanebooks.com

1   3   5   7   9   10   8   6   4   2

Text © Angela McAllister 2008
Illustrations © Daniel Howarth 2008

The right of Angela McAllister and Daniel Howarth to be identified as the author and illustrator of this
work has been asserted by them in accordance with the Copyright, Designs and Patents Act, 1988.

A CIP record for this title is available from the British Library.

ISBN: 978-1-86233-724-4

Printed and bound in Indonesia

Santa's Little Helper

Angela McAllister • Daniel Howarth

GULLANE
CHILDREN'S BOOKS

Rufus was a fidget.
He chattered and giggled and
skipped and tumbled all day long.

He couldn't keep still when his brothers were building in the snow.
He couldn't keep quiet when his sisters were listening to a story.

He was the most fidgety arctic hare there ever was.
"I can't help it," said Rufus. "I just get excited."

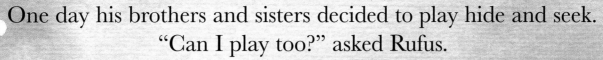

One day his brothers and sisters decided to play hide and seek.
"Can I play too?" asked Rufus.
"Yes," they said, "if you can keep **very still** and **very quiet**."
"I promise," said Rufus, bouncing up and down
happily. "You'll see, I won't twitch a whisker!"

He set off to find a good place to hide.

The first place
wasn't far enough.

"I might just need to
scratch my ear," thought
Rufus, "and then they
would see me."

So he went further.

The next place
wasn't far enough.

"I might just need
to hum a little hum,"
thought Rufus, "and
then they would
hear me."

So he went further . . .

And further . . .

And further . . .

At last Rufus found a perfect place to hide.
A wriggly, giggly excitement fidgeted inside him.
But Rufus remembered his promise.
He tried as hard as he could to keep still and quiet.

Rufus waited and waited and waited and
waited. But nobody came to find him.
He was so still and so quiet that
after a while, he fell asleep.

Rufus didn't hear footsteps crunching through the snow.
"Ho, ho, ho!" a voice chuckled. "I nearly left these behind."

Rufus was put into a sack full of presents
and carefully lifted onto a sleigh.

He woke to the sound of jingle bells
and a deep voice humming a merry tune.

Rufus peeped out . . .
The starry sky spun around him.
The wind whistled through his whiskers.
"I must be dreaming!" he gasped.

Then the sleigh
landed with a bump . . .

Rufus tumbled
out into the snow!

"Hello there, little one," chuckled
Santa Claus. He picked Rufus up.
"I thought you were one of the toys!"

"Would you help me?" he asked. "There is so much to do."
Rufus nodded happily.

There were lots of presents to carry, and stockings to fill.

And as Rufus helped, he chattered and giggled
and fidgeted with excitement . . .

. . . and nobody minded at all.

At last all the sacks were empty.
"Thank you," said Santa Claus. "What a good thing
you're so lively! We finished early with your help."
He gave Rufus a special Christmas present.
"Now we'd better get you home!"

Rufus climbed up into the
sleigh beside Santa Claus. He
was so tired, he fell fast asleep
as the reindeer galloped
through the night sky.

He didn't even wake up when Santa Claus
laid him down gently outside his burrow.

Next morning his brothers and sisters found him.
"Where did you hide?" they asked. "We looked everywhere."

"I was so still and so quiet I fell asleep," said Rufus
with a yawn. "But I had a wonderful dream!"

"Well, you won't have to be still and quiet today,"
said his brothers and sisters. "Come on! We're going sliding."

"Hurray!" cried Rufus. And, as he ran happily after them
through the snow, the jingle of a tiny bell told him
that his Christmas dream was true!